Pooh's Pumpkin

Disney's
Winnie the Pooh First Readers

Pooh Gets Stuck
Bounce, Tigger, Bounce!
Pooh's Pumpkin
Rabbit Gets Lost
Pooh's Honey Tree
Happy Birthday, Eeyore!
Pooh's Best Friend

Disney's
A Winnie the Pooh First Reader

Pooh's Pumpkin

by Isabel Gaines

ILLUSTRATED BY Josie Yee

DISNEY PRESS

NEW YORK

Pooh's Pumpkin

One sunny spring day
Pooh and Christopher Robin
saw Rabbit planting seeds
in his garden.

"Rabbit," asked Pooh,
"what are you planting?"
"Pumpkin seeds," said Rabbit.

"I would like to grow
a pumpkin, too," said Pooh.
"A growing pumpkin
needs special care," said Rabbit.

"I will take good care of it,"

promised Pooh.

Rabbit handed Pooh a seed.

Pooh and Christopher Robin
found a sunny spot
near Pooh's house
to plant the pumpkin seed.

"I will sit here
and watch the pumpkin grow,"
said Pooh.

"But Pooh,"
Christopher Robin said,
"the pumpkin will not be
ripe until next fall.
That's a lot of sitting!"

"My pumpkin
needs special care," said Pooh.
"And that's just what I will give it.
But first I have to get
something to eat."
Pooh went into his house
and gathered all of his honeypots.

Then he went back outside
and sat with his honey.
He watched the spot
where the seed was planted.
He watched and ate,
and ate and watched.
And spring turned into summer.

In the middle of the summer,
Piglet stopped by.
"What a pretty vine
you are growing, Pooh!"
he said.

"Oh, but Piglet,"
said Pooh sadly,
"I wanted a pumpkin,
not a vine."

17

Pooh went on caring for
the vine.
At the end of the summer,
a flower was on the vine.
Pooh was looking
at the flower
when Owl stopped by.

"Pooh, your flower
looks just right.
Keep up the good work,"
said Owl.
"Oh, but Owl," said Pooh sadly,
"I wanted a pumpkin,
not a flower!"

"Pooh, I will be happy
to tell you
what you are growing.
You have a vine.
You have a flower.

A flower grows on a vine
before there is a . . . cucumber!"

"You are growing a cucumber,"
Owl stated.

"Oh my," Pooh said.
"I wonder if cucumbers
taste good with honey?"

"Think, think," said Pooh
to himself.
"Rabbit gave me a pumpkin
seed. So it should grow
into a pumpkin.
I will keep caring for this plant
and see what grows."

Pooh went back to work,
watching the plant
and eating his honey.
From time to time
the ground seemed dry,
so he watered the plant.

One day the air was cooler.

The leaves were just beginning

to change colors.

Pooh had fallen asleep.

He woke up with a start.

Eeyore was standing over him.
"There is a green ball
on your vine," said Eeyore.
"Oh, Eeyore!" said Pooh sadly,
"I wanted a pumpkin,
not a cucumber,
and not a green ball."

"Oh, well," moaned Eeyore.
"I suppose we can find
something to do with it,
whatever it is."

Days and weeks passed.
The green ball
grew bigger and bigger.
Pooh's tummy was growing
bigger and bigger, too.

One morning Pooh saw
that a small part of the ball
had turned orange.
As the days went on, it became
more and more orange.

Then the air got cooler
and the leaves fell from the trees.
And on Pooh's vine was a huge
orange pumpkin!

Everyone gathered around Pooh
and his pumpkin.
They looked from Pooh
to the pumpkin
and from the pumpkin
back to Pooh.

"That pumpkin looks just like
your tummy, Pooh!"
laughed Tigger.
"Silly old bear," said
Christopher Robin.
"You gave the pumpkin
so much care
that you grew along with it!"

"Let's all carve the pumpkin
into a jack-o'-lantern,"
said Christopher Robin.
Owl carved the eyes.
Rabbit carved the nose.
Piglet carved the mouth.

Pooh's pumpkin was
the best jack-o'-lantern
in the Hundred-Acre Wood.

Join the Pooh Friendship Club

A wonder-filled year of friendly - activities and interactive fun for your child!

The fun starts with:
- Clubhouse play kit
- Exclusive club T-shirt
- The first issue of "Pooh News"
- Toys, stickers and gifts from Pooh

The fun goes on with:
- Quarterly issues of "Pooh News" each with special surprises
- Birthday and Friendship Day cards from Pooh
- And more!

Join now and also get a colorful, collectible Pooh art print

Yearly membership costs just $25 plus 15 Hunny Pot Points. (Look for Hunny Pot Points on Pooh products.)

To join, send check or money order and Hunny Pot Points to:

Pooh Friendship Club
P.O. Box 1723
Minneapolis, MN 55440-1723

Please include the following information: Parent name, child name, complete address, phone number, sex (M/F), child's birthday, and child's T-shirt size (S, M, L)
(CA and MN residents add applicable sales tax.)

Call toll-free for more information
1-888-FRNDCLB

Fun for kids ages 3-8

Help your child learn
MATH and READING
with a computer and
a silly old bear.

©Disney

sɴᴇʏ's Learning Series on CD-ROM

 our child on the path to success in the 100 Acre Wood,
Pooh and his friends make learning math and reading
isney's Ready for Math with Pooh helps kids learn all the
tant basics, including patterns, sequencing, counting,
eginning addition & subtraction. In Disney's Ready to
with Pooh, kids learn all the fundamentals including the
bet, phonics, and spelling simple words. Filled with
ing activities and rich learning environments, the 100
Wood is a delightful world for your child to explore
and over. Discover the magic of learning with Pooh.

Wonderfully Whimsical Ways To Bring Winnie The Pooh Into Your Child's Life

Pooh FRIENDSHIP

Pooh and the gang help children learn about liking each other for who they are in 5 charming volumes about what it means to be a friend.

Pooh STORYBOOK CLASSICS

These 4 enchanting volumes let you share the original A.A. Milne stories — first shown in theaters — you so fondly remember from your own childhood.

Pooh PLAYTIME

Children can't help but play and pretend with Pooh and his friends in 5 playful volumes that celebrate the joys of being young.

Pooh LEARNING

Pooh and his pals help children discover sharing and caring in 5 loving volumes about growing up.

FREE*
Flash Cards Attached!
A Different Set With Each
Pooh Learning Video!
* With purchase, while supplies last.